All About the Sky

CeCe Wilson

Rosen REAL READERS

Rosen Classroom™
New York

The sky is the color blue.

The sun is in the sky
during the day.

The clouds are in the sky.

At night the sky is dark.

The moon is in the sky.

The stars are in the sky.

Words To Know

clouds

moon

stars

sun